Turtle Dolphin Dreams

A Work of Metaphysical Fiction

By Marian K. Volkman

First Edition: April 2005 (ISBN-13   978-1-932690-10-1)
                              (ISBN-10   1-932690-10-7)

Library of Congress Control Number: 2005902290

Distributed by:
Baker & Taylor, Ingram Book Group, New Leaf Distributing Co.

Published by:
Loving Healing Press
5145 Pontiac Trail
Ann Arbor, MI 48105
USA

http://www.LovingHealing.com or
info@LovingHealing.com
Fax +1 734 663 6861

Loving Healing Press

Loving Healing Press

You Are Invited

To read the story of how this book came to be written

To read about the author

To read the short essays:
"Animal Intelligence and Inter-Species Communication"
and "Nature in Balance"

Or to participate in a potential book project, visit

www.TurtleDolphinDreams.com

Also by Marian Volkman:

Life Skills:
Improve the Quality of Your Life with Metapsychology

www.LifeSkillsBook.com

$1.00 from the sale of every
Turtle Dolphin Dreams book
has been donated to Greenpeace
(www.greenpeace.org)

Acknowledgements

First, thanks to all of the people who wrote books and made videos from which I learned a lot about both turtles and dolphins. (For a list of some of the books I found useful including books on animal intelligence and inter-species communication, see my book list by visiting www.TurtleDolphinDreams.com and clicking on the "book list" button.

I have had enormous amounts of valuable help on the manuscript of this little book from my husband, Victor Volkman, my sister Jennifer MacLean and my friend, Michele Rae Vierra. Thanks also to Peter Szabo and Robert Rich, Ph.D. for valuable critiques.

For encouragement when it was needed most I thank my daughter, Stephanie Dreher, my cousin Katherine Gasciogne, and friends Christine Hucker, Irene Szabo, Tammy Greco and Annie Hannan.

Tremendous thanks to the brave people of Green Peace for all they have done to protect the oceans and life on our planet. Thanks to individuals and groups working to raise the consciousness of humankind on the subject of all life on our planet. Thanks to everyone who is mindful of our relationship to this planet and the other species with whom we share it in all its beauty, abundance, and fragility.

Special love and thanks to my husband, Victor, for all of his support, expertise, and encouragement.

About the Art

Front cover art by Sudee Taormina

Interior illustrations by Marcus Dillon (pages: 2, 4, 7, 16, 17, 18, 22, 28, 37, 39, 44 & 51)

Additional sketches by the author

Space photographs by NASA

Creative director for the book cover design, Victor R. Volkman

Contents

Part One – Beginnings

I, a Turtle, address you for reasons and through means which I will endeavor to make plain. I have messages for you, but if I throw them out in front of you like pebbles on the sand, you may not see them. This is why I ask that you be patient as I explain both how I come to be speaking to you (it must be obvious to you that a Human has a hand in this), and why.

You may wonder who I am. You may feel the need of a name for me, the Human informs me. My impulse, and Turtles are not impulsive creatures for the most part, is to ask you to pay attention to the messages I bear you instead of to me. Upon sober reflection, and Turtles are sober reflectors, it may be best for me to introduce myself. I will not tell you whether I am male or female, but you may know that I am the sort of Turtle who spends part of its life in the water (in ponds and streams), and part of its life upon the land (in forests and fields), and who hibernates when the cold season comes. Many a summer has awakened me. Many a winter has drawn me down to sleep.

If you need a name for me, think of me as Turtledove. Of course, this makes no sense. A turtledove is a type of bird. I am not a bird, but my companions, of whom you shall hear, chose this name for me because it is pretty and graceful (which, believe it or not, is how they think of me) and non-gender-specific. So be it. To the task awaiting us.

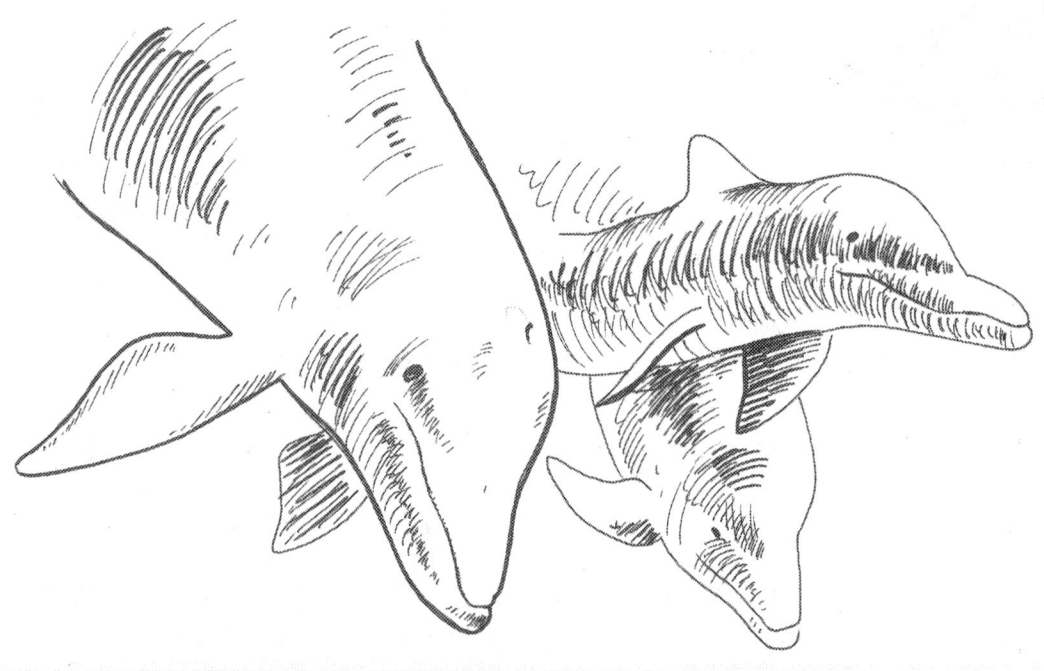

I come to you, through these symbols, to bring you communications from another highly intelligent, highly complex life form. That is plain enough. How this can come about is another matter. Since you know that Turtles can neither speak your language nor write it, you might find this communication difficult to believe if I did not spell out each step of its coming to be. A group of Dolphins wishes to speak with you in order to share their view of the world contrasted with what they understand of your own, and to propose some joint activities. My part here is to help in the effort to formulate this work, so that you may see and receive it. Even now we have no certainty of success, but we must try. You are probably far more interested in what the Dolphins have to say to you than you are in my humble part in this attempt to reach you, but please indulge me by taking the time to understand how this work comes to be attempted.

Were it not for a special state we call dreaming we would have no chance of communicating with you (and by "we" here, I mean both Turtles and Dolphins). Dreaming to Turtles meant at first something very similar to what it means to you: the entering of consciousness into a state of mental activity while the body rests. Over time it began to mean for us something more fully conscious, and eventually came to mean *dreaming together*, entering into a state of non-physical awareness with others of our kind. We must go back several steps for you to understand how you come to be reading this work. We will start with the time when Turtles dreamed only on a primitive level.

We Turtles (and I speak here only of the number of species of my kind that I know well from dreaming/communing with them) have two modes of existence: summer and winter. In summer we live and work and

grow as all creatures do, finding food, mating, and traveling as Nature calls upon us to do. There is no time for dreaming during the summer days, when we are fully engaged in physical pursuits. Even as we lie basking in the sun for hours, storing up the warmth it seems, to see us through another winter, that time is full, full of the scent of water, the sensation of heat, the feeling of comfort from having eaten our fill. It is a physical focus, a physical time.

Swimming, of all summer activities, provides the experience closest to dreaming as we glide freely, almost without effort, anywhere in water-space that we choose to go, a far different experience than walking is for us, with our short legs and heavy shells. The swimming sense of easy motion and fluidity is similar to dreaming, yet still the physical sensations demand all of our attention: the caressing water streaming past our limbs, the sheen of light at the surface, the soft cool mud in the murky depths, our bulky shells turned weightless.

When winter comes, we hibernate. It is a deep, deep sleep, unlike the drowsy, partly conscious sleep of summer. Closed off from the physical world as if dead, with nothing to distract us, we dream.

I suppose we must always have dreamed, as long as there were Turtles in winter, Turtles in deep, deep sleep. We must have dreamed, otherwise sinking down into the mud and entering the state of hibernation would be too claustrophobic, too much like dying. Even so, the transition is a kind of death. Each winter we die to the physical world and enter the dream world. Each summer we must leave dreaming behind, die to that existence, and come up into the sun again, back to the pains and delights of physical being.

Turtles are by Nature solitary creatures. We tolerate companionship while sharing a basking log in a pond for instance, but except for this casual association, and of course the brief but intense occasions of mating, we tend to be loners. Our relationships are neither close nor of long duration. All of this is true at the physical level of existence, but slowly a change came to pass in the dream world.

Our dreaming was limited at first to the things of the physical realm, the sort of dreaming common to almost all sleeping creatures: fear, flight, food, and delight. At some point in our development Turtles learned, through the length and depth of our winter sleep, to dream together, conscious of ourselves and of each other. We began to be able to commune together, to play with thoughts, and to gain as much enjoyment, though of a very different kind, as we get from swimming, eating, mating, and basking in the sun.

From generation to generation we grew in this ability. Of course all of this history is not part of my personal memory, but we have a way, perhaps related to the ability to dream, of feeling back through time, through the generations, to know of events and developments which occurred far back in Turtle history.

One winter, many generations ago, a group of Dolphins came to us in the dream world we thought to be our own. Though surprised to be so invaded, most of the Turtles were not displeased. They learned then to make a choice whether to enter into, common dream-space as it were, or to stay behind in our old dream-space. There are some who prefer to stay with the old ways. While many of us delight to dream with Dolphins, there are Turtles who dream only with Turtles, and some who dream only with members of their generational line. This is as it is and therefore as it should be.

The Dolphins who came to us during our winter dreaming have taught us much and expanded our horizons to the limits of the very planet itself. Does this make us reluctant to feel the summer call us forth once again? Not at all. The power and freedom of swimming is a joy without parallel for Turtles. A full stomach feels as satisfying; the warmth of the sun on one's shell feels as comfortable. There is balance in everything, but let me not get ahead of myself.

Perhaps all sleeping creatures dream (in the sense of telepathic communing) at some time and to some extent. This I do not know, but apparently few kinds of creatures dream with the depth, completeness and certainty that Turtles do, probably because hibernation allows us to give the activity our undivided attention. Far beyond our level of dreaming are our friends, the Dolphins and their cousins, the Whales. Cetaceans (your other name for Whales and Dolphins), have evolved to the point where they can dream and wake at the same time. Unlike us, they have no need to remove their attention from the physical realm in order to reach the state of dreaming. They can dream even while swimming.

Many a winter has passed in deep communion between us, those of us who choose to enter into it, and the group of Dolphins known to us. The wonders they have shown us are far beyond anything we could have imagined. "And why should they bother?" you might ask. I have wondered myself, for though they take evident pleasure in communication for its own sake, we Turtles have nothing as vast in our experience to share with them in return.

It was not only to bring us into communication for our own sakes though, that these Dolphins sought us out. Their intuition led them to realize that our unique characteristics might help to form a link between themselves and the Two-Legs, as we Turtles call you, a link over a gap which heretofore had been unbridgeable. This is not to make light of the occasional close friendship formed between individual Dolphins and individual Humans over the centuries, but this group of Dolphins seek more with you than friendship. They seek communion, deep and true.

While these Dolphins are interested in communicating and communing with as many other species as possible, they feel a special urgency to reach you. Two-Legs have a unique impact on the planet.

They have a purpose or mission to draw into communication every species who is willing and able. For some it represents quite a leap. There are some species on this planet who like to believe that they are the only ones who matter.

Have you ever wondered what the Whales and Dolphins are doing with their very large and complex brains? Some of you have wondered. From the Human perspective, such advanced intelligence as Whales and Dolphins may possess is wasted since they do not produce *things*. No physical structures or objects, no machines or art works, no visible culture is left behind from one generation to the next.

Though the different species within Cetaceans do not necessarily co-habit peacefully, there is a fair amount of inter-species dreaming. From the perspective of the Cetaceans, the great intelligence of Humans is wasted in the production, distribution and busy rearrangement of *things* to the extent that Humans seem to be distracted from the vital occupation we call dreaming.

If you have wondered how Whales and Dolphins occupy their great minds and brains, we will tell you ("we" being this linkage coming through to you now of one Turtle, one Dolphin and one Human). This race of highly intelligent creatures sharing a planet with you live in an environment so foreign to you and with culture and occupations so strange to you, that they might as well be invisible. Whales and Dolphins in their various societies have been engaged for many centuries in philosophy and art, and other subjects you may feel some strain to believe. (We thought of mentioning science, understanding science to be the study of what is, and how it works, but the methods of Human study are so different from Dolphin study that we decided it is best not to call them by the same name.)

In addition to these occupations, for countless generations Whales and Dolphins have tried to communicate with you in many different ways. Some of these attempts have even been recorded in your books, but in spite of that, they have attracted little notice from Humankind. Within the relatively recent past, a particular group or association of Dolphins has been trying, not through physically observable methods such have been tried in the past, but through the dream state. Though all Whales and Dolphins dream, we are reserving the name "the Dreamers" here for that special group.

The belief that you are the only truly intelligent creatures on this planet has gotten in the way of your receiving their communications. For those of you with a fascination with the idea of encountering strange and different races from other planets and attempting communication with them, we invite you to look upon similar fascinating challenges and possibilities with your planet-mates.

Part Two – The Dreamers

These Dolphins, the Dreamers, wish to reach out to you because of a kinship they feel for you despite the profound differences between your frames of reference, they being sea creatures and you being land dwellers. Frame of reference proves to be a crucial point. For all of their efforts to communicate with you, the application of their intelligence, will, and heart, no satisfying progress has been made. Some few people who have studied Dolphins closely have come to understand some part of what we are telling you here. These Humans tend to be scoffed at by their fellows. This is what we mean by saying to you that no real progress has been made in establishing communication with you beyond the level of proving that Dolphins are capable of learning tricks and games taught by Humans.

This is where we Turtles come in. I, Turtledove, address you. We are not the only creatures to hibernate (which gives us long experience of the dream state), but we have other characteristics that fit us for the task at hand. We are water creatures who walk upon the land. Does it seem like overstating the case to you, to call ourselves water creatures, when we are air-breathers like yourselves?

Consider the Birds. They also walk upon the land, but they are creatures of the air. If they could not land to rest, they could not live, just as if we could not come up for air, we could not live, but a Bird is most intensely alive when it is flying. Turtles, slow and plodding on the earth, are most intensely alive when we swim. (This is why we do not refer to birds as "Two-Legs", though they have these appendages, but as Creatures Who Swim in the Air.)

These very contradictions of ours, that we are not only land-walking water creatures, but also deep-dreaming physical creatures, enable us to perform the function, at least potentially, of bridging the gap between Humans and Dolphins. Land-walking I have in common with you. Swimming I have in common with the Dolphins. I live half my life as a day-to-day, moment-to-moment physically-oriented creature, such as you Humans tend to be. The other half of my life I spend dreaming, in deep telepathic communion with other Turtles and the Dreamers.

The Dreamers live much of their lives in the state of super-conscious, thinking-togetherness that we call dreaming. Let us not forget that though they are air-breathers too, the Dolphins live all their lives in the water. This is difficult to conceive of even for us, water creatures that we are. How much more difficult to comprehend it must be for land-walking creatures such as yourselves?

"Wait," you may be saying, "what about Turtles who live in hot dry climates, who do not swim, who never experience winter and do not hibernate?" Yes, they exist, and though they are Turtles, we cannot reach them, cannot dream with them as we do with the Dreamers, despite the fact that they are our own kind of animal. Now are you beginning to understand the challenges that face us? Apparently it takes both our abilities to swim and to dream for us to be able to enter into dream-space with the Dolphins to the depth of communion and clarity of understanding that we have achieved together.

The Dreamers theorized, and it appears to be true, that since we also spend significant portions of our lives walking upon the land as you do and immersed during that time in physical pursuits to the exclusion of dreaming, we would make good candidates for helping to establish a link with you. This proves to be more difficult in practice than in theory.

The Dreamers know much more of you than you do of them. They are able, through practice, to enter into rudimentary dreaming/communing with some of you when you are asleep, meditating, or in some other very quiet restful state. At these times the Dreamers see your world through your own mental constructs. Much of what they see does not make sense to them, except as they are occasionally able to guess from your feelings and emotions connected to the images.

As we Turtles can, the Dreamers can feel back along their genetic memory. They tell us of a time when their ancestors, those of both the Whales and Dolphins, walked upon the land. This memory is so faint and far-distant however (it was long before Humans' appearance on the planet, for instance) that it provides them with no clues to your world. Through sharing perceptions with a receptive dreaming Human, they have seen certain things from your point of view. They have seen the huge, sharp-edged dry reefs in which many of you live, but cannot understand them. (They have passed these glimpses on to us, who comprehend them even less than the Dreamers do.)

Once they conceived of Turtles' potential to help increase understanding between Humans and Dolphins, the Dreamers set to work to realize this potential. Though "work" seems too serious a word to use in connection with these most playful of beings (here our Dolphin partner in the link transmits great leaps and splashes) we use the word to convey the strength of their intent in this endeavor.

More than one generation of Turtles has participated in the effort, those of us who are interested in the project by reason of our communion with the Dolphins. The Dreamers communicate to us such of your experience as they can receive, asking that we translate as best we can from land-walker concepts to water-dweller ones. Then they put across to us the ideas they most wish to communicate to you, so that we can attempt to translate back the other way. This is very hard for us to do. In this work we do not use words as you know them, but concepts, pictures and feelings. This is a rough explanation, but as close as I can come to explaining the process.

We know the Dreamers well, as we are both water creatures, and have dreamed together for so long. Then again, the Dreamers do not harm us but have brought us great richness of experience, while the Two-Legs have hunted, captured, confined and tormented many of us for generations beyond counting. At first we could not believe that Dolphins, who have suffered even more at the hands of Two-Legs than we Turtles have, would wish to enter into communion with such a species. It took a great deal of gentle persuasion on their part to convince some of us to help. At first we were persuaded on the grounds of trying to preserve Life on this planet. Some of us have worked most of the winters of our lives on this project. Through this work we have at last come to feel some reluctant affinity for you.

The next phase was to try to bring a Human into the project. In this very long time, only one complete link has been established and developed to the point where a physical transcript can be attempted. We have been fortunate enough to find a Human, very experienced in the art of meditation, who could set aside the constraints of purely physical reality and commune with us. We have learned that only one individual from each of the three species can be part of the link; otherwise already difficult communication becomes hopelessly garbled. The group of Dolphins engaged in this has chosen one of their number to speak for them (though they are able to be in such close telepathic connection that the rest of the group can "listen in" without upsetting the link.)

The choice of Human was easy, since we have only found one individual in a position to take on the job, which is to say with not only the ability, but also the time and free attention to work concertedly with us. There is in fact a race of Humans with whom Dolphins have dreamed for many generations; however, this race is so little regarded by the dominant races of Humans that they have been ignored at best; at worst hounded and marginalized nearly to the point of extinction despite their great virtues. Despite the fact that they are Human, they have had almost insurmountable difficulty in trying to communicate with the rest of you so we, the members of this project, could not ask them to take on this task, but had to find another person to try to make our message heard. The Human who writes to you now is long-practiced in meditation and other spiritual efforts (the Dreamers would say not "efforts" but "games", but do not wish to trivialize this individual's... efforts).

Our Human partner is apparently one of many of you who has made a leap by seeking and learning along spiritual paths. This appears to be a period of great spiritual upsurge. Meditation has been thought to take extended periods of disciplined time and effort to eventually reach a desirable state. Some of you are discovering that you are able to reach the desired state quite rapidly and that you have no interest in continued practice beyond that point, at least for that day. This new form of rapid meditation, if we might call it that, has proven helpful for this work you are reading now. There is nothing wrong with the old ways, so please do not feel in any way wrong or diminished if you practice them. If, however, you are one who finds yourself able to achieve deep levels of peace, which is to say, fine high levels of vibration, in a matter of minutes or less, please do not feel that you are lazy or incorrect if you do not spend great amounts of time in practice. The Dreamers see the result of meditation or other spiritual practice as being much more important than the method.

The three of us have agreed, upon consideration, that we will not reveal to you the gender of any one of us. This may make for some awkwardness of expression, the Human tells us, but we feel the message is better served if any gender bias is eliminated. The depth of dreaming-together makes each participant able to share the experiences of other individuals, should those individuals choose to share them. Therefore male Turtles know what it is to lay eggs. Male Dolphins know what it is to give birth. Female Turtles and Dolphins can feel distinctly male experiences. Please feel free to think of us as any gender you wish. We will not be offended.

This is less a linear linkage than a circular one, a sort of conference call, according to the Human. The purpose of the work is to let the Dreamers have an open channel to you at last. In this way they can share some of their ideas and hopes, and can invite your interest and participation in this fascinating activity.

(Here our Dolphin companion transmits a series of extravagant leaps, with and without splashes, to convey enthusiasm.) Although intent and serious upon this business, as serious as Dolphins ever are, our friend at times becomes so exuberant that nothing will do to express this strong emotion but the telepathic sending of it in the form of Dolphin acrobatics. The Human and I receive these transmissions almost as if we were able to leap and dive and tail-walk upon the water ourselves. Words do not express the strong feeling (usually unbounded joy), of these spatial exclamations, but we will inform you of them nonetheless, so that you may receive at least some idea of this Dolphin's expression.

The Human wishes to remain anonymous and as unobtrusive as possible and is making every effort to merely translate and transcribe without adding to the message, though it will inevitably come across as a Human-sounding communication (or how could you receive it, after all?). It is my wish also, to convey the Dreamer's communication to you in as pure a form as possible, but the Human succeeds far better than I do. Forgive me. I can only think in my own terms and to a limited extent beyond them as revealed by the Dreamers.

It is my honor to be the Turtle in this link. Since I am nearing the end of my life, there is some urgency to commit this effort to a form that you can receive. It takes the individuals of the link a long time of striving together before the work begins to come together.

Near the beginning of our three-way dialog, the Human wished to ask some questions of the Dreamer. As they may be questions you would want answers to, that conversation is included here. The first question was: "Are you all enlightened?" The Dolphin replied, "No, as in your world, there are some who live without thinking."

As the Human has conceived through the link that the Dreamers sustain a rich culture of forms of expression which might translate in Human terms as dance, music, and sculpture (this being projected with sound you might say, rather than engraved upon material objects), the next question was, "Are these forms of expression created and then lost, or carried down somehow from one generation to the next?" The Dreamers are unable to comprehend the meaning of this question. Next the Human wanted to know, since the Dolphins' arts take the same form as their day-to-day communications with each other, "How do you tell the two, art work or communication, one from another?" The Dolphin's answer was, "How do you tell yours apart?"

Finally then, the Human asked if the Dreamers are aware of Humans' music, dance, art forms, and philosophical thought. The Dolphin's reply to this was yes, (executing a very splashy double leap followed by a high jump and a silky-quiet dive) they are aware of some of it and that this, most of all, makes them wish to communicate with you on a much deeper level than has ever yet been achieved.

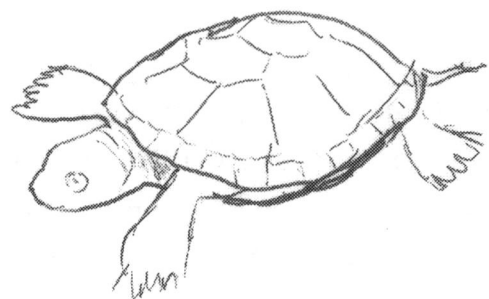

I, Turtledove, will make one further remark, before we progress. Left to myself I would never have thought of myself as simple. My life, to me, is rich and full. However, through close communion with a Dolphin and a Human, each in their different ways creatures of marvelous complexity, I see that I am simple. This is no fault, or lack in me. We Turtles are as Nature made us. The length of our tenure upon the planet (far longer than either Humans or Dolphins), is testament to the success of our design. However, this difference in our degrees of complexity offers a further challenge to our communication which is almost enough to make me despair of the attempt. Many subjects I can only approach from my own frame of reference. Only the Dreamers could have persuaded me that my efforts will be good enough to serve the purpose. Whether they are good enough is for you to judge.

Part Three – Relationships

There are great differences in the experiences of Human, Dolphin and Turtle, in how we relate to others of our kind, in how we reproduce, and so on. Such considerations may seem to you to be irrelevant, but our comprehension of the nature of Life Itself is based on such a major philosophical difference that I cannot get past it without sharing the Turtle perspective on these things. By showing you the Turtle viewpoint, I hope that you will better understand my communication. In addition to that, the Dreamers themselves have admired and learned from Turtle wisdom in the matter of relationships. They think that you may also learn from us.

Perhaps the most primary of all relationships are those of the generational line: parent-child / child-parent. This we deduce from the patterns of our dreaming. In the physical realm, Turtles form no close associations between parents and children. Remember that we are hatched from eggs buried in the earth by our mothers, not born alive as are Humans and Dolphins.

For Dolphins, family bonds are enormously important and form the basis for their society. (Here the Human and I are made to feel the powerful sensation of a pod of Dolphins swimming together: a ballet of interconnected motion.) Particularly in the Dolphin female line, strong associations hold from generation to generation as mothers, aunts, and sometimes grandmothers, aid daughters in the birth process and the care of infants. If a mother dies, there is always a female relative, usually appointed at its birth, to take over care of the young one who is left behind.

Though Dolphins' mating is tender, intense, joyful and absorbing, like Turtles, they do not mate for life. (Please note that though Humans generally claim to mate for life and seem to see a special virtue in this, the facts are often otherwise.) Turtles are seasonally driven to mate and in most cases easily satisfied, while most Humans and Dolphins seem to be driven regardless of the season.

Once a Dolphin or a Turtle has mated with another, that individual's essence imprints indelibly upon that partner. From that time forward, the dreaming-together of those two individuals has a special quality, though in the physical world they may go their separate ways. In fact, Dolphins say that dreaming-together for them originated in the intense coming together of mating. For us Turtles, dreaming-together originated as a phenomenon of our solitary winter's sleep, but the first individuals we were able to contact in the dream state were our parents, children, siblings or former mates.

Contrasted with the impermanence of most mating, one's offspring are always one's offspring, one's parents are always one's parents. This connection for Humans apparently can cause both greatest joy and greatest sorrow.

While we labor to understand this, we Turtles return again and again to our notion of the generations, each one created in eggs, laid whole and complete in a nest of sand or loamy soil, hatched among our siblings, but without an adult in sight. This clear division between the generations seems to us a desirable thing. We well know now that mammals cannot reproduce in our way. Your young leave their mother's body, prematurely we would think, without the benefit of a protective shell. Weak and embryonic, they depend upon your good will and your continuing efforts on their behalf for their survival.

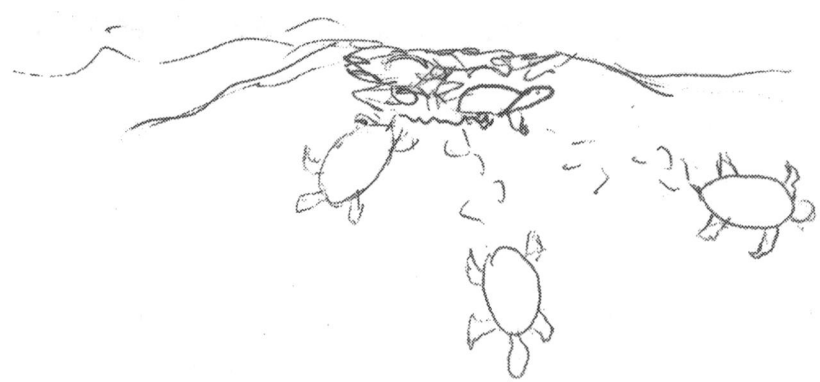

A female Turtle, after fertilization by her mate, creates whole perfect eggs within her body. Full of the weight of those eggs, she must dig a nest in the ground, lay those eggs, then cover them up. Once done, drained but satisfied, she walks away.

Those of our children who survive their first summer enter into dream-time. Whenever we "encounter" them there, we recognize our mark upon them, our essence mirrored in them, and know them as our own. We have no telepathic connection with our children before they enter into their first winter. Hence we are spared the pain of knowing their fate if they are eaten by predators, either as eggs or new hatchlings.

We understand that newborn mammals have desperate need of care and that their parents are driven by Nature to care for them. We understand that a Dolphin male will fight to the death to protect the young of his group and that a Dolphin mother gets enormous pleasure from association with her young one. While both Human and Dolphin mothers suffer intense and lasting pain at the death of a child, Humans appear at times to suffer almost comparable pain from their living and thriving children. This we cannot understand. Human parents and offspring continue in close association, necessary due to the dependence of the children, for many seasons. During this association they derive from each other small or great amounts of pleasure, and inflict on each other small or great amounts of pain.

Of course, you cannot lay eggs as we do, lay eggs and then walk away from them. Your young cannot be expected to be, as ours are from the day they are hatched, independent, self-sufficient creatures. That is not their nature, but perhaps you would benefit if you could conceive of your children as eggs for a moment, whole and perfect, separate and complete, beings unto themselves, without attachment to you. Of course they need you. That is without question. But see them whole for a moment. See their life as their life.

Each life is an egg, we often think. Each individual Turtle's life is a unit, a whole, just as the organism itself is a unit with boundaries and limitations. For us, our skin and our shell set our boundaries, but we also live within the limits of our senses and capabilities: the distance we can see, hear and smell, how fast we can swim, how far we will walk in a summer season, how long we must hibernate in winter, how many summers and winters we will know before we die.

The "egg" of a life starts when we first break the shell as we hatch. It is circumscribed by the limitations of our physical living as creatures upon the land and in the water. Death is the far edge of the shell of life. This is not sad (though we Turtles, as all living things do, strive to live as long as we can as Nature bids us to do). It is completion and wholeness. A life would be nothing without its limits and boundaries. The same limitations do not apply in the dream state, but on the physical plane, too much desire for "everywhere-ness" may lead to a lack of connection with "here-ness" and "now-ness", we feel.

It must be difficult for you to conceive of your child as an egg when it was born naked, conscious of the world around it, and able to look into your eyes. For this reason, we Turtles ask you to back up a step or two and look at each Human life, yours, your mate's, your child's, your friend's, as an egg. Your lives overlap each others' with great intensity in a way that ours do not, but surely you can grasp this idea.

If you can be aware of the separateness, the complete-unto-itself "egg-ness" of each life, this awareness may spare you pain. Of course, your life will still overlap with the lives of others. There will be influence and interchange, but no matter how much of this influence there is back and forth between you, each life is still an egg. If you see your child (or your mate, or your friend) as an extension of you, and that individual takes *actions that you would not take*, you may experience this as pain. If you see each other person you encounter, no matter how closely associated with you, not as an extension of yourself, but as a creature whole and separate from you, you may approve or disapprove of his or her actions, but that will not, we believe, cause you so much anguish.

You are the center and sovereign of your life. "You-ness" pervades every aspect of your life. You may have a great impact on the lives of your parents, your mates, your children and your companions, but only you are the common denominator of your life, through and through, whole, complete and perfect like an egg. Can you see it?

For better or worse, you touch and influence the lives around you, but if those individuals were not here (if they happened to be born, let us say, on the other side of the planet), you would still be you. Though you would lack the "flavor" or "color" of your association with those individual Human Beings, there would be others taking their place, adding their colors to your life. On the other hand, if you were the one to not be here, to be born on the other side of the planet, your associates still would be themselves as individuals, whole and complete. Can you feel it?

The struggle to express this is greater than the struggle to hatch. I must rest.

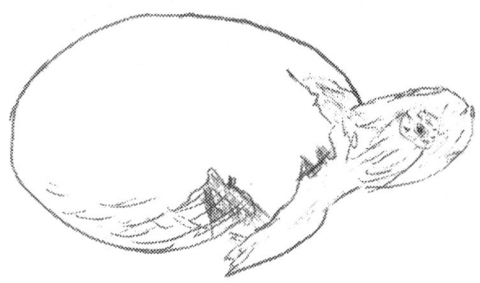

My companions remind me that we need to speak of relationships within the context of dreaming. From the Turtle point of view, relating to others of our kind while in the dream state is like swimming together, but swimming more closely than our shells would ever allow in the physical state. It is a liquid, flowing, moving-without-moving closeness. Knowing another Turtle in dream-space is like "knowing" water or air; each is experienced directly and purely. This purity of the dreaming-together experience can come as a shock, delightful or otherwise I am told, to more complex beings like yourselves.

We are all naked in the dream state.
We neither have, nor need shells to protect us.
You neither have nor need pretended feelings, pretended identities.
Dolphins are strangers to both shells and pretense.

The Dreamers have become aware through their intensive efforts to understand you, that some Humans have deep fear of relationships on such a level. These individuals flinch at the idea of fluidity and defenselessness. If you feel such a fear, the Dreamers hasten to reassure you on several points: (Our Dolphin here performs a soothingly gentle maneuver, swimming just at the surface and looping slightly over and under the water in a relaxed curve, more beautiful to experience than to describe.)

Do not fear to lose your identity. You are always you. Just as you might swim more easily without clothes on, you may find that you will dream more easily without the "clothing" of certain mental or emotional attitudes. You are no less yourself without your clothing (though the Human feels that some may argue this point!) Likewise, the essence of you is not dependent upon various attitudes you may have assumed in moments of stress or down-heartedness.

Do not fear "falling into" the dream state. It takes a conscious decision, and on the part of most Humans, the application of practice and discipline to achieve. Short of ingesting foreign substances, which is not recommended, you will not "fall in".

Do not fear "melting". From the physical perspective, it is difficult to think coherently about the phenomena of the dream state. How shall we say this? The forest is the forest. We may feel it as an entity, yet every tree in the forest is, as itself. In the dream state, you may share space and consciousness with another, or even many others, to a degree impossible in terms of these bodies we inhabit, but do not fear. You will not lose yourself.

On the spiritual plane, we are able to overlap, inter-lap, we might say, even as the waters of the world do. Things that would be contradictory at the physical level are not contradictory here. Separation and connection, unity and interdependence may flow together and nothing is lost. (Our Dolphin executes seemingly effortless great curving leaps and dives to illustrate this point.)

As we contemplate the subject of relationship, we see that the two apparently contradictory concepts: life as an egg (Turtle concept), and life as fluid motion (Dolphin concept) - have much to offer each other. In respecting myself as whole and complete, I respect you in your wholeness. In respecting you, the "egg" of your life, your space, your identity, I respect myself. As an individual feels secure in his or her identity and uniqueness, that individual becomes able to move past physical boundaries and enter into deep communion with others, without fear of ceasing to be. In being able to flow together and share dream-space, each of us is refreshed in our experience of our unique self.

As is often the case according to Dolphin wisdom, a seeming paradox holds a treasure of deeper understanding. The "sides" of the paradox are like two halves of a clam shell, which are tightly joined together. Inside is the treasure. In this case, one side is: "Separateness is good." The other is: "Togetherness is good." Thus it is that Dolphins love to find a paradox to play with. They delight in communicating with other kinds of life forms who may have very different views than their own, for such communication is productive of new paradox shells.

Part Four – Food and Other Pleasures

Dolphins always and Turtles usually eat our food alive. We have come to understand that to you this may seem cruel or barbaric. (Long discussion was needed for us to comprehend the concept of "barbaric.") From our point of view, our living food is able to enjoy its life up to the moment when we require it to continue our own survival. Living creatures they may be unhappy about being eaten, but Nature has provided such creatures for us to eat, and we must eat to live. In addition, live food brings us more Life. Both Turtles and Cetaceans in captivity are forced to eat dead food, a great diminishment in the quality of our lives and a partial explanation for the fact that we do not live as long in captivity.

Your food is called upon to die considerably in advance of your consuming it. This may not be wrong or unnatural for you. Many types of creatures store food, spiders, for instance.

A message the Dreamers wish to convey to you, is that to them, pleasure and Life are almost synonymous. (Here our Dolphin dives deep, then shoots up high past the surface of the water with a great frisking of the tail.)

Of course, painful things can befall a living creature, even horrible and apparently senseless things such as captivity and torture; however, Life as it should be is pleasure itself. The definitions of these things cause difficulty. The Human tells us that many of your kind feel that their pleasure depends upon accumulating things. This concept is entirely foreign to us. We look forward to learning from you concerning this matter. It may well be as good for you to accumulate things as it is useless for Turtles and Dolphins to do so. We do not mean to criticize you. We bring up this point only as it represents an obstacle to our understanding of each other's assessment of what in Life has value.

It may be that Dolphins are not taken very seriously as highly intelligent life forms by Humans because not only do they not busy themselves in collecting objects, but they also spend so much time at play. (Our Dolphin friend embellishes this discussion by demonstrating great prowess at racing through the water at enormous speed, then braking to a fast stop. This performance concludes with a leap and a deep dive.) The Human explains to us that play for you is relegated to childhood, not that adult Humans do not play, many of them do, but most of them feel the need to develop complex justifications for spending time at play. This is utterly beyond Dolphin comprehension. We (both Turtle and Dolphin) wonder if we misunderstand this state of affairs, but the Human assures us that we do not. Please note that to Dolphins the concept of "spending time" has little meaning. The Dolphin tells us that according to their understanding, time in itself has no value.

To take a moment for a simply Turtle point of view, we spend a great deal of time in what Humans would consider idleness when we bask in the sun, but this is not play. (Neither is it idleness, to our way of thinking.) Swimming Turtles may seem playful, and maybe they are, but there is usually purpose to us in swimming beyond the pursuit of pleasure, or entertainment... Be patient with me please, as I struggle to understand.

Ah! Now I feel it. Turtles truly play only when we are in the dream state. *That* is play!

All right now, let us attempt a more precise statement of Human play. For children, play is all about learning how to live. Dolphins see the activities of their young, though often playful, as serious practice, getting ready for the rest of life. Dolphins feel that only when this intense learning phase is through and the young Dolphin has reached adulthood can it afford the free attention needed for real play. Play for Human adults seems to be considered as activity with no... tangible reward. (Things again.) You may also consider play to be a sort of active idleness. Perhaps you feel that it is activity with no purpose other than the activity itself.

Now we may be getting closer to the crux of the matter. The Dreamers understand play as very close to Life Itself. Physically sustaining activities, such as eating, trying to avoid being eaten, mating and care of the young, all of which Dolphins are driven to do as well as you are, only comprise part of Life.

The other part, the greater part, Dolphins see as play, not in the sense of idleness, mere entertainment or purposeless activity, but as (how shall we put it?), mental food, spiritual food, if you will. The play of a Dolphin nourishes, informs and delights that animal's spirit. You have observed that even in captivity (a state no one, Human, Dolphin, or Turtle prefers) Dolphins play. One who will not play drifts close to death.

We humbly suggest that you consider the Dreamers' point of view in this matter. The young are playful, it is true, but consider how much they must learn! Their play is of necessity more serious and limited than that of an adult, who has learned how to live and now can turn attention and curiosity loose in free and far-ranging play.

Play, pleasure, Life Itself: these things are part of a single whole in Dolphin consciousness.

Of course, land-walkers have some pleasures which water-dwellers cannot feel, the pleasant feeling of solid ground under foot, for example, but some sorts of experience please more than one kind of creature. Dolphins and Humans for instance, have the pleasure of skin against skin as two living creatures touch to commune with each other. Whether they be friends, lovers, or parent and child, the touch of that loved one's body can bring deep comfort and satisfaction.

All three of us in the link have felt the special pleasure of breaking through the water's surface after a long dive, the sparkling aliveness of taking in Life-giving air, only to dive deep again into the caressing, Life-giving water. The pleasure of eating, so good in itself, also brings the bodily senses of contentment and strength: the readiness to move as we will.

Beyond all this, if we can stretch our awareness to encompass it (and for us Turtles, that requires dreaming) the Dolphins say that there is the living creature's pleasure in the sense of rightness in the order of the world. We feel it in day following night, the progression of the seasons, our planet's place in the universe: a world so innately friendly and sustaining to us all.

Common life activities done in a playful, open, receptive spirit give pleasure, but what about play for its own sake? For Dolphins, a form of play involves objects they find (a use of things, I note!) playing for instance with a feather or a bit of wood to watch how it moves in the water. Dolphins love to see how things in the natural world affect each other, continually forming new patterns though they follow certain laws. Observation of natural law and of what you call chaos theory fascinates them.

Dolphins play at stretching and leaping, even shooting their bodies up above the surface to "tail-walk" on the water. Such sport is play and play is Life. The Dreamers understand that your games may be similar in essence to their own, though yours have more rules.

Play extends to other life forms for the Dolphins. They play with Fish, with Eels, all sorts of creatures, including Humans! A Dolphin has even been known upon occasion to play games with a Sea Turtle. They find another sort of play in interaction with their own kind, a special sort since Dolphins are so telepathic: love play, bossy play, long distance communication play, creation of art forms play.

The most complex form of play for the Dreamers (hard to explain, since it pervades all other forms of play and Life Itself) is balance, used in this sense to mean the consideration of Life with a global perspective. It took the Dreamers many, many generations to develop this form of entertainment. Individual Dolphins long, long ago were aware only of themselves, and of other individuals with whom they dreamed. Out of that kind of connection perhaps, or maybe out of the strong close love of family members for each other, grew eventually the awareness of the interconnectedness of all Dolphins and eventually Whales as well. After many generations of dreaming together, this group, the Dreamers learned at last to start reaching some other types of creatures in the dream state.

When they first entered into communion with land-walkers, (Turtles to be precise) they felt their consciousness take a further leap. Each individual so linked in the dream state now had the ability to sense our world with a global perspective: land, water and surrounding air. The planet itself, the Life which inhabits the surface of the sphere, and the inter-connected strands of that Life became "visible" (in a dreaming sense).

Having achieved this perspective, Dolphins went on to learn to sense ecological trends: balances and imbalances between the moving tides of the various sorts of energies and life forms surrounding the planet. The Dreamers experience this sort of thought as play because it uses all of their abilities to sense, to hold and juggle concepts, and to predict. (This might be called "science" for the sake of seeking truth and knowledge, distinct from research aimed at producing physical results.)

Please note that our Dolphin wishes, from apprehension about losing your willingness to continue to receive this communication, (diving deep and shaking its whole body from side to side) to omit from this message a fact which burst unavoidably upon the consciousness of all three of us while working on this subject. The Human and I determine to include it, nonetheless.

In observing trends in the web of Life over the surface of the planet, we see that while the number of Humans alive today increases at a rapid pace, the numbers of Turtles and Dolphins alive today dwindle almost as quickly.

We are, each and all, interconnected with every living thing on this planet. Every living thing. Do you doubt it? Well you may. Turtles, with our shell-enclosed, often solitary existences, could not conceive of such a thought were it not for the dream state and our work with the Dolphins. Because of their enormous capacity for dreaming, dreaming-while-waking as we might call it, and their abilities to enter into dream-space with other species than their own, the Dreamers often swim in this awareness of planet-whole interconnectedness. Maybe some of you have a sense of this.

Here we will attempt direct communication from the Dolphin, to the best of our combined ability.

Pardon us now as we speak of less than happy subjects. Doing so only makes sense because these are the things which inhibit play, pleasure and Life Itself. If we wish to experience Life to its fullest, we need to face up to that which prevents the full enjoyment of it. As living creatures are able to experience pleasure, they also experience pain. Pain, on the individual level or beyond, tells us that something is wrong in the flow of Life Itself. Pollution causes illness and death among all of us, Humans, Turtles and Dolphins alike. By pollution we mean all that discords with Life as it should be, caused by mixing substances with the air, water, or soil, intentionally or by accident, which render them unfit for use by living creatures.

Those of you who do this sort of mixing must have a reason for these activities which we cannot fathom and which must seem greatly important to you, otherwise why would you take such risks? Please consider whether the reward for these activities is worth the pain. Besides directly causing and contributing to many fatal ills, pollution diminishes the general state of wellness in all it touches.

We would include in this subject of pollution something our Human told us of: the use of artificial substances which grow you fine-looking food with poor content. The Dreamers cannot understand and ask you to look earnestly upon this situation.

Some of you, distressed by the level of serious illness in your population, look to your food as a cause of your pain. Through long and earnest study and exchange of information with our Human, we believe we comprehend the problem. The harm comes in food altered from Nature, grown without proper nourishment so that it can in turn nourish you, or contaminated with substances which allow it to be stored for long periods without "spoiling." Dear Humans, it is already spoiled! It is not-food.

We do not wish to point a finger at Humans on the subject of health or rather lack of health. Do Dolphins never ail? Of course we do. In fact, Dolphins share some of the illnesses Humans use to demonstrate mental and emotional superiority to other animals. We too may suffer stomach ulcers in high anxiety situations. We also can have heart attacks. Yes, we contemplate future consequences of current actions and may worry about them. Dolphins grieve when separated from their loved ones. Like Humans, they can even turn to suicide when despair becomes too great. (Suicide has been thought by Humans to be a uniquely human aberration, and evidence of intellect.)

Our purpose here in speaking of pollution and illness is not to blame, but to engage with you in contemplation of pleasure and Life as it should be, for you, for us and for all of Nature's creatures.

Dolphins have some qualities that you have not fully developed, as you have some which they have not. Some Humans almost worship Dolphins and this worries us. We are not perfection. We are what we are. Please do not idealize us. (Swimming in a large slow circle.)

As an example of something you might consider a fault in Dolphin character or behavior, they are sometimes rougher than you would think appropriate during courting games. Males can be pushy with females, and also with each other. (Certain Whales are even rougher and have fierce battles among themselves.) Keep in mind that these games are only between Dolphins, and are part of their social structure. A Dolphin has had, upon occasion, to push a drowning Human fairly hard to get them to safety, but this has usually been well understood by the drowning Human!

Back to pleasure. Ideally all of Life should feel like play, not a giddy sort of escapism, but play in the sense of adventure, discovery, humor, surprise, and full satisfied enjoyment of the activities of being alive. Humans pride themselves upon their intelligence, perceptiveness and inventiveness. The Dreamers ask you to indulge yourselves by developing that combination of traits to its fullest, to cherish the spirit of play as you cherish Life Itself.

Admittedly, your lives are very different from ours. You need shelter and clothing. You need to store food. You record your art forms in matter. (Dance and music, live, not written down, are the closest things to shared art forms between Dolphins and Humans.) Despite these differences we are sure that you can apply your great intelligence to this:

How to live fully, joyfully and abundantly in balance with the natural world.

Some of you see this challenge as a grim task. You may find it easier to consider this life-long project as a form of play. (Exuberant arabesques: twirling, curling leaps and plunges.)

This the Dreamers wish ardently, not only for the sake of all species alive on the planet, but also for the sake of your happiness. We wish you the joys of play without ceasing. We wish you the balance, harmony and freedom that come with play in the fullest sense of the concept, as individuals, in your groups of family and friends, and as a species in relation to other species. With this harmony, we believe, will come a greatly enhanced ability to dream.

Part Five – The Seam

In their efforts to understand you, the Dreamers have come to realize that you perceive the place where water and air meet to be a division of elements, a separation of worlds. Because they live out their lives immersed in water yet breathing air, what you see as a division, we see as a connection.

Try for a moment to feel this from the point of perception of a water-dweller. (Shooting above the surface to tail-walk on the surface, then slipping below again to swim strongly in an arc.) Of course Dolphins are aware of the difference between the two elements. No one could be more aware of that difference than air-breathing water-dwellers, but as large bodies of seawater and the air above them are both necessary for our survival, we see them as two parts of one world. Air and water form a whole in our conception. As we move back and forth within these two great elements, the line of their meeting we may call the Seam.

We wonder whether your seeing the two parts of the world so separately explains a behavior of yours which has been in the past incomprehensible to us. When you put waste material into bodies of water, it may seem to you that you have put them sufficiently "away" from you as to be no longer a part of your world. Is this so?

If the two great elements were completely separate, not "stitched", as the Human says, together: some water in the air, some air in the water, there would be no world as we know it, and we would not be addressing you. Imagine, if you will, swimming and breathing, swimming and breathing, not as an exercise or sport, but as Life Itself. Dolphins swim and breathe, swim and breathe, stitching the Seam, rejoicing in it, every day of our lives. (Long loopy rolling dives into the water, into the air.)

As air and water are different, and their coming together can be seen as a seam, let us look at the coming together of other differences in this way. Male and female are different, yet they belong together. This is not meant to diminish the joy and power in relationships of all kinds between male and male, or female and female, but neither all the male individuals, nor all the female individuals of most kinds of creature can carry on the race. Both are needed. You may look at the difference as a dividing point, a battleground even, or as a coming together that forms a seam.

This is the stuff of Life Itself. The coming together of two un-likes allows for a profound learning, sharing and exchange, whether the "un-likes" be physical elements, male and female, race and race, or species and species. We may even take this thought down to the level of the coming together of any two individuals. No matter how alike they may seem from outside observation, each living creature is a discrete, separate entity with its own skin, its own identity, its own life, an egg, as the Turtles say. This is true enough. Each individual remains itself even in relation to others. Yet in the wider world, the shared world, each living creature carries around it its zone of influence. Here living creatures come together to share experiences and to create, or attempt to create, effects upon each other. The coming together of any two creatures creates a seam.

Ocean and air teach us by their coming together. In sensing our difference from each other, our uniqueness, yet reaching out to deeply know and understand another, we form not a division, but a seam. This knowing of each other creates a larger whole of you-and-me, a little world unto itself. As each being is unique, so is each relationship between beings. This meeting and connection can give living things joy, enthusiasm, and contentment: Life as it should be.

We are all interconnected in the same way that molecules of water in the oceans are. There is no changing that. In addition to this impersonal sort of connection, we have the potential to bond with others in a more conscious way. We are bound to have seams with those living close to us. Beyond those connections are the ones we bring about by seeking out others to know and care for. These others may be like us, kindred spirits, or they may be intriguingly different and hence attractive to us in their very unlikeness. (Enthusiastic splashing!)

What holds the universe together? The attraction of particles to each other: large and small, tiny and huge, wet and dry; that, but also the seaming of individual Beings, one to another, for better or worse.

What is "for worse" you may ask? A seam, our Human has taught us, may be sewn badly, which can pucker and mar the larger fabric. What constitutes a poorly sewn seam in terms of relationship? A puckered seam in a relationship can come from resistance to the connection and from unwillingness to fully know another's viewpoint, (by which we mean, to understand in the fullest sense, not necessarily to agree). Another sort of problem with seams comes from individuals acting not in the present moment, but from some past confusion of pain or fear, so that that one or both the participants do not perceive the other clearly in the now. How in that case could we hope for a seam well-sewn?

An individual who lacks certainty of his or her own essence may fear being taken over by another's personality and so may resist, which prevents knowing. Contrarily, some individuals, unsure in their own being, try to remedy that lack by pushing into the space or being of others, dominating or invading. These ills (for so we see them) prevent potentially beautiful seams from coming to be. We living things pull and strain at connections we don't like, but we may tear ourselves in the process.

Having looked at "for worse," let us now consider what constitutes "for better" in these connections. A good seam between individuals, which needs to be well-sewn by each, makes us more complete, more fulfilled, more enlightened and delighted for knowing the other. (Forward flip, making a nearly perfect circle cutting through air and water.)

Water and air interweave, some air in the water, some water in the air. In doing so they help each other to sustain Life, each in its way. If one or the other is polluted, it shares its burden of pollution with the other. Can individuals share "pollution" through the seams between them? Of course they can. How is this to be prevented or remedied? The only way we know to do this is by rejoicing in the seam itself, perfecting the connection and interchange. This includes taking the care and attention to smooth out the puckered places, which are caused by misunderstandings and failures to truly know the other.

Seaming is not a simple act (though certainly one Being can know another whole and complete in the flash of a moment, especially in the dream state). The creation of a seam between two living organisms is ideally a long and delightful process as the two come to know each other more and more purely, deeply and truly, without resistance, without attack or defense, without either enveloping the other or holding aloof. This exercise calls upon all of our strengths and abilities.

To reach you, I must be able to be still deep within myself. I must know myself. For our relationship to live, both of us must continue to deepen our knowledge of ourselves and of each other. I am I, thee are thee, and this living shining thing between us is our unique connection.

Part Six – New Beginnings

Come dream with us.

The longing is great. Many of you have tried, but sometimes in ways that prevent the best quality of communication possible between us. A relationship based on capture and confinement is unlikely to move, flow and grow as it could if based on freedom and equality. (Let us make note of something here. You might assume that the ability to dream-together with loved ones would be a comfort to a captive Dolphin, but in fact the stress of captivity itself and of living in an unnatural environment obscures most or all of a Dolphin's capacity to dream.)

Your coming into the water with Dolphins, though it can be enjoyable for all concerned, may actually get in the way of true communion. You are not water creatures. Try as you will, you cannot live comfortably in water as we do. This is not meant to invalidate the sincere attempts some of you make to come to us, to reach us. We treasure and embrace the spirit of these attempts.

We ask you now: come to us in your mind, in your spirit. Dream of us, waking or sleeping. Meditate deeply, using any practice or method that you choose. That will help you to reach dream-space where we can commune together.

Some of you are willing to work very hard to reach us. Now here is a paradox for you: by all means use whatever mental, emotional and spiritual exercises you can, by whatever custom suits you, but if you would reach us, learn also to play lightly.

Play lightly: how can we best express it? Here are some examples of Human activities (gleaned through careful work with our Human) which may be as valid and valuable as deep meditation, we think:

❖ The moment when, while sharing food with friends, you look around and feel that you love them, a deep contentment.

❖ The time when you are with family, not a hard-driving, accomplishment-oriented event, but a period of leisure, being together by chance or design, feeling the comfort of your kin around you.

❖ All the moments when you experience the natural world through clear eyes, clear senses:

    o See a Dragonfly shimmering its iridescent way about its business.

    o See a mosaic of translucent autumn leaves, hear a waterfall in a warbler's song.

    o See fir trees lift their dark wings against the sky.

    o Feel silky water or silky air flow past your skin.

    o Watch any birth or hatching.

    o Feel the great pulse of Life in a large body of water.

All of these moments when you receive joy and light-heartedness in profound stillness of spirit bring you closer to true communication with us. Please do make the time in your lives for such moments. Some of you think of it as laziness, but those quiet times, quiet states of peace and contentment, can be the very thing to bring about special states of awareness. Of course it would be stupid to starve for lack of catching Fish. There is work to do in life, but if we learn to love the work we do and to leave plenty of time for playfulness, quietness and receptivity, then we truly live.

Is the purpose of our dreaming together merely the pleasure and fulfillment it would give? No, though that would be enough, there are other reasons.

We feel Life on other planets calling to us. Some of you feel it too. We are amazed at your courage as you have expended tremendous effort to fling yourselves into the sky. We are also amazed that you do not seem to match the effort you exert on the physical plane (not that we see anything wrong in such effort) by a similar attempt in the mental/spiritual realm.

Dolphins jump high out of the water, but lack the means you have to shoot your bodies far above the surface of this planet. Lacking that avenue to reach out to Life beyond this world, we have long attempted to reach it directly, telepathically. Only the faintest sensing comes through.

Lately we have realized that perhaps we cannot reach living creatures on other planets until we succeed in our effort to enter into full communication with you. Now we believe that when we fully know each other, together we will be able to know the galaxy.

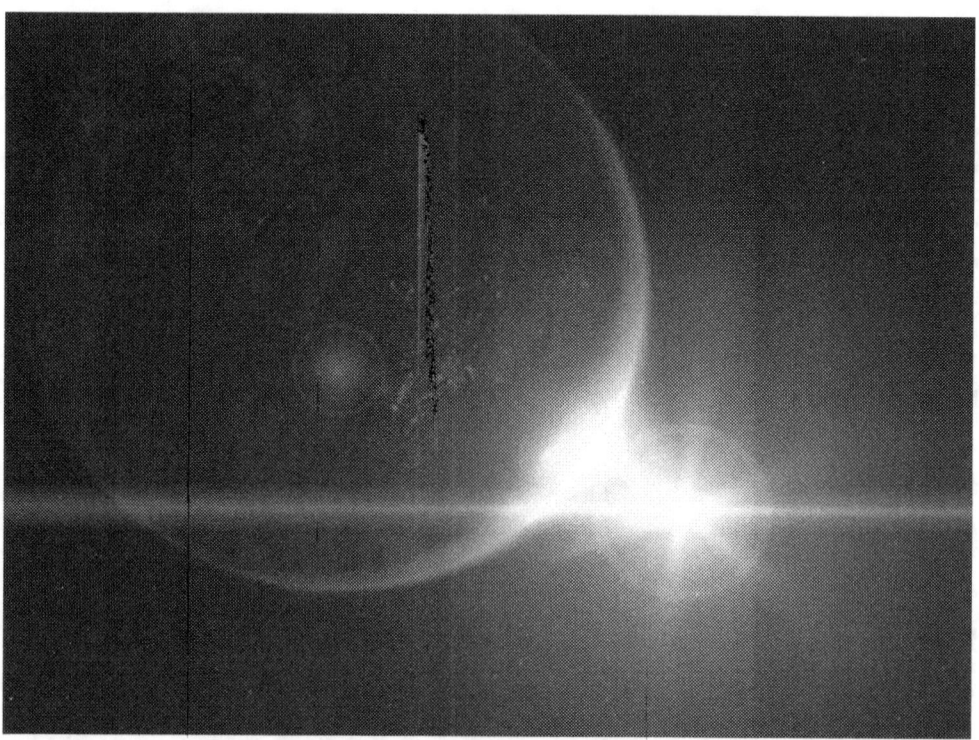

For many seasons now we have felt a great building of spirit, of consciousness toward some sort of coming shift or transformation we can only guess at. We know that some of you feel it too, more and more of you as this wave builds. Where it will take us we do not know, any more than you do. We strongly feel it, that together we are meant to do far more than we can do in isolation from each other. Where this may lead us we do not sense for certain, but the possibilities fill us with enthusiasm. (Loud smacking tail whacks upon the surface of the water.)

Sometimes in meditation or other spiritual exercise, in sheer joy of living or in pain of seeking, you reach out strongly and touch Dolphins as they dream. Sometimes the Dreamers have brief flashes of dreaming-together with you. In these times they do not sense that you feel them as what they are, Dolphins, but that you interpret the contact in various ways. They have been surprised to be thought of as "angels".

Does this mean that there are no angels? Of course not. We keenly feel the presence of Beings-without-bodies. There are many types. Some have the behavior and thought processes of Fish while others have the presence and intellect of Whales. Sometimes we can communicate with them, but not as clearly as we would wish. Again, we need you. In fact, some of you have greater facility we think, for this communion with Be-ings-without-bodies than we do.

There is a bit of confusion to clear up in the section just covered. "How is it," the Human wants to know, "that Dolphins recognize Humans while dreaming but Humans (even allowing for the fact that they are gen-erally less adept at dreaming) fail to recognize Dolphins when they make contact in dream-space?"

As we three work this out, Humans generally move in two dimen-sions, firmly grounded. Beings-without-bodies are only located in a physical sense by the point from which they choose to view or experience something. If they decide to shift their location, they may do it in one hop, as it were, or in a fluid motion in any direction. So even with style of loco-motion as their only clue, Dolphins could distinguish between Human Beings and Beings-without-bodies in the dream state. The fluid motion method more closely resembles swimming than it does walking upon the land, so a Human, upon contacting a fluidly moving Dolphin in the dream state, with whom it shares little context in mode of travel, or a fluidly mov-ing Being, may experience these contacts as similar.

We need you. BE with us. Come dream with us!

Epilogue

I, Turtledove, address you:

The sun is starting to warm the land again, and to pull me back into my body as this work draws to a close. It is with cautious satisfaction and a little sadness that I bid you and my link-mates good-bye. I am thankful for the profound experience of working in the link. I hope that these messages will reach you in good season, and touch your heart.

The Human and Dolphin are united in the wish that this be called Turtle Dolphin Dreams, in respect for my part in the work. I question their wisdom in this, seeing the work as primarily Dolphins' communication to Humans, but they insist.

Thank you for attending to this communication. It is the wish of all of us in the link that it may find you in good health and good spirits and that it may cheer your way onward in this Life we share.

www.ingramcontent.com/pod-product-compliance
Lightning Source LLC
Chambersburg PA
CBHW080544180626
46818CB00008B/3120